Dear Parents and Educators,

Welcome to Penguin Young Readers! As parents and educators, you know that each child develops at their own pace—in terms of speech, critical thinking, and, of course, reading. Penguin Young Readers recognizes this fact. As a result, each Penguin Young Readers book is assigned a traditional easy-to-read level (1–4) as well as an F&P Text Level (A–P). Both of these systems will help you choose the right book for your child. Please refer to the back of each book for specific leveling information. Penguin Young Readers features esteemed authors and illustrators, stories about favorite characters, fascinating nonfiction, and more!

The Lucky Dogs
Penny and Clover, Up and Over

LEVEL **1**

F&P TEXT
LEVEL **C**

This book is perfect for an **Emergent Reader** who:
- can read in a left-to-right and top-to-bottom progression;
- can recognize some beginning and ending letter sounds;
- can use picture clues to help tell the story; and
- can understand the basic plot and sequence of simple stories.

Here are some **activities** you can do during and after reading this book:
- Character Traits: Clover is a dog, like Penny, but she and Penny have different traits. Write down a list of words that describe Clover.
- Sight Words: Sight words are frequently used words that readers must know just by looking at them. They are known instantly, on sight. Knowing these words helps children develop into efficient readers. As you read the story, have the child point out the sight words below.

and	come	it	me	up
can	good	jump	not	you

Remember, sharing the love of reading with a child is the best gift you can give!

D0170171

To rescue dogs everywhere.
And to the lucky people who take them
into their hearts and homes—ESP

For Dani, with all my love—LM

PENGUIN YOUNG READERS
An Imprint of Penguin Random House LLC, New York

Penguin supports copyright. Copyright fuels creativity, encourages diverse voices, promotes free speech, and creates a vibrant culture. Thank you for buying an authorized edition of this book and for complying with copyright laws by not reproducing, scanning, or distributing any part of it in any form without permission. You are supporting writers and allowing Penguin to continue to publish books for every reader.

The publisher does not have any control over and does not assume any responsibility for author or third-party websites or their content.

Text copyright © 2020 by Erica S. Perl.
Illustrations copyright © 2020 by Penguin Random House LLC. All rights reserved.
Published by Penguin Young Readers, an imprint of Penguin Random House LLC, New York.
Manufactured in China.

Visit us online at www.penguinrandomhouse.com.

Library of Congress Cataloging-in-Publication Data is available upon request.

ISBN 9781524793418 (pbk)   10 9 8 7 6 5 4 3 2 1
ISBN 9781524793425 (hc)   10 9 8 7 6 5 4 3 2 1

Penny and Clover, Up and Over

by Erica S. Perl
illustrated by Leire Martín

Come on, Penny.

Come on, Clover.

Jump like me.

Jump up and over.

Good dog, Penny.

Come on, Clover.

Jump like Penny.

Up and—

Clover.

No.

Not that way.

Come on, Clover.

You can do it.

Up and over.

Up.

Up.

Up.

Up and—

Over.

Clover did it.

Good dog, Clover.